W9-AVX-201

To Paree Hartley with thanks

Angus&Robertson
An imprint of HarperCollins*Publishers*, Australia

First published in Australia by William Collins Pty Ltd in 1980
Reprinted in 1981 (twice), 1982
First published in paperback in 1982
Reprinted in 1983, 1984, 1985, 1987, 1988, 1990
This Bluegum paperback edition published in 1991
Reprinted in 1992, 1993, 1994 (twice), 1995, 1996, 1999, 2000
by HarperCollins*Publishers* Pty Limited
ABN 36 009 913 517
A member of the HarperCollins*Publishers* (Australia) Pty Limited Group
http://www.harpercollins.com.au

Copyright © Pamela Allen 1980

This book is copyright.
Apart from any fair dealing for the purposes of private study, research,
criticism or review, as permitted under the Copyright Act, no part may
be reproduced by any process without written permission.
Inquiries should be addressed to the publishers.

HarperCollins*Publishers*
25 Ryde Road, Pymble, Sydney NSW 2073, Australia
31 View Road, Glenfield, Auckland 10, New Zealand
77–85 Fulham Palace Road, London W6 8JB, United Kingdom
Hazelton Lanes, 55 Avenue Road, Suite 2900, Toronto, Ontario, M5R 3L2
and 1995 Markham Road, Scarborough, Ontario, M1B 5M8, Canada
10 East 53rd Street, New York NY 10022, USA

National Library of Australia Cataloguing-in-Publication data:

Allen, Pamela.
Mr Archimedes' bath.
For children.
ISBN 0 207 17285 4.
I. Title.
823'.3

Typeset by Savage & Co Pty Ltd, Brisbane
Printed in Hong Kong by Printing Express Ltd
on 128gsm Matt Art

19 18 17 16   00 01 02 03

MR ARCHIMEDES' BATH

PAMELA ALLEN

Angus&Robertson
An imprint of HarperCollins*Publishers*

Mr Archimedes' bath always overflowed.

And Mr Archimedes always had to clean up the mess.

"Can anyone tell me where all this water came from?"

Mr Archimedes decided to find out.
He put just a little water in the bath,
as he always did, and this time
he measured the depth.

But the water rose.

"Where did all this water come from?"
bellowed Mr Archimedes.

"I don't know," said Kangaroo.

"It's not my fault," said Goat.

"I didn't do it," said Wombat.

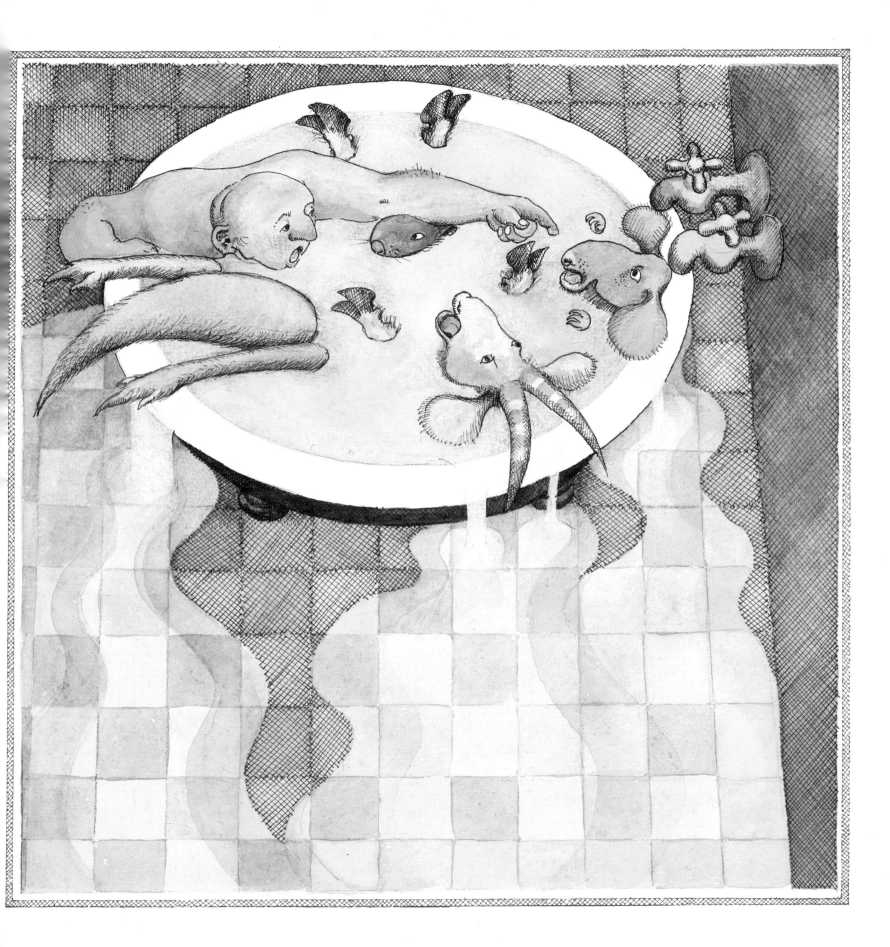

But when Mr Archimedes measured it again, he found the water had gone down. Mr Archimedes was puzzled.

"Somebody must be doing this," he shouted. "Where's it gone?"

"Maybe it is you, Kangaroo.
You stay out and we shall see
if it happens again."

The water rose.

When Mr Archimedes measured it, he found it had gone down again.

"Now let's see what happens when you are left out, Goat."

Again the water rose.
That left only Wombat to blame.
Mr Archimedes was angry.
"Get out and stay out," he shouted.

But the same thing happened.
Who could be responsible if it
wasn't Kangaroo and it wasn't Goat
and it wasn't Wombat?

Could it be Mr Archimedes?
The friends decided he should have
his bath all to himself.
He climbed in,

and the water rose.

He climbed out, and the water fell
until there was just the same amount
Mr Archimedes had put in.

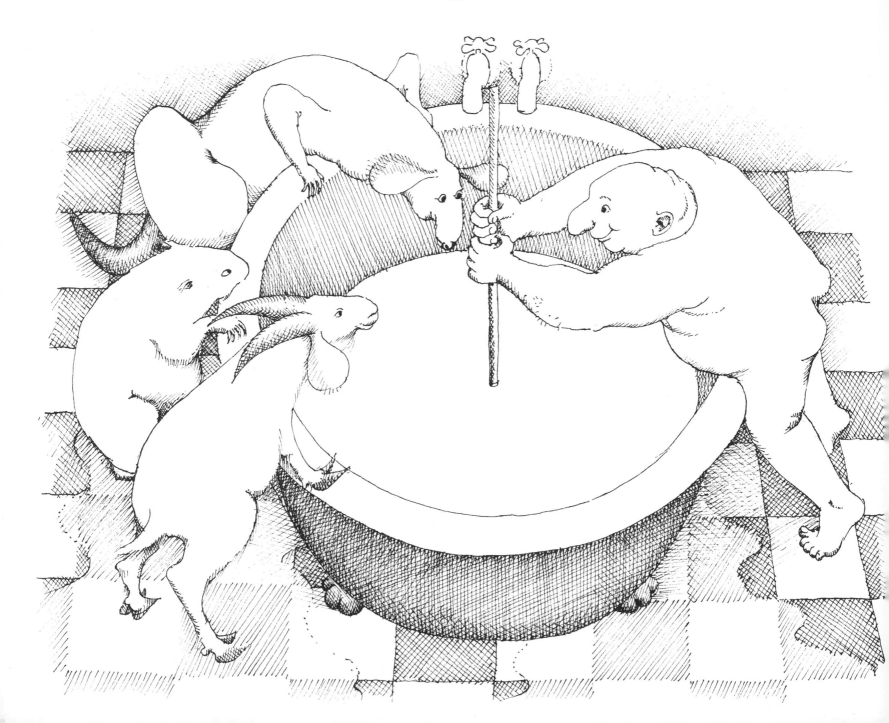

Mr Archimedes got so excited that
he jumped in and out, in and out,
to make the water go up and down.

"EUREKA!

I've found it, I've found it!" he shouted.

"Jump in everyone!"

And the bath overflowed.

"See," said Mr Archimedes.

"*We* make the water go up.

There are just too many of us

in the bath, that's all!"

The friends had so much fun that night,
jumping in and out, making the water
go up and down, that they made more
mess than ever before.